UNBREAKABLE

Our life journey with brittle bone (OI) condition

By

Tarela Aghanti

www.tarelaaghanti.com

First Edition Published by Tarela Aghanti

Copyright ©2020 Tarela Aghanti

My WOW Moment

All rights reserved. Neither this book nor any parts within it

maybe sold or reproduced in any form without permission.

No part of this book may be reproduced in any form or by any

electronic or mechanical means including information storage

and retrieval systems, without permission in writing from the

author. The only exception is by a reviewer, who may quote

short excerpts in a review.

The purpose of this book is to educate and entertain. The views

and opinions expressed in this book are that of the author

based on her personal experiences and education. The author

does not guarantee that anyone following the techniques,

suggestions, ideas, or strategies will become successful.

The author shall neither be liable nor responsible for any loss or damage allegedly arising from any information or the suggestion in this book.

Dedication

I dedicate this book to God Almighty, to every person living with brittle conditions globally, to my amazing son Steven, with whom I have this journey. To my parents Eng. Richard G. Ovia and late Emily Yere and to every Osteogenesis Imperfect (OI) organisation across the globe, working so hard to raise awareness on the condition and finally to all the OI professionals supporting others globally.

Love

Tarela Aghanti

Author Forgiveness is Key

The Inner Secret to a Healthy Life

And

Unbreakable

Our live journey with brittle bone (OI) condition

Thank you for purchasing a copy of my book, "Unbreakable" Our journey with brittle bone condition.

Tarela Aghanti

Table of Contents

CHAPTER 1

LIVING WITH BRITTLE BONE (OI) DISEASE	29
Different Types of brittle bone (OI) disease	31

CHAPTERS 2

FACING YOUR FEAR	40
Feel free to talk about it	44
Be truthful with yourself	45
Self-Love/Acceptance	45
Forgive yourself	48

CHAPTER 4

Springing forth with a child with OI/disability	56
Your peace	59
Feeling worthless and shame	62
Regret, unwanted feeling	64

CHAPTER 3

TRADITION & CULTURE	69
Different stages of African wedding	70
Pre-Marital Introduction Ceremonies	71
After-Birth Care	73

CHAPTER 5

GRANDMA CARE/Treatment	79
What is Grandma care or grandma treatment?	80
My Opinion	85
My experience with grandma's care treatment	88
Ignorance is a disease, but knowledge is Power	88

CHAPTER 6

BELIEF & FAITH	102
Religious Jargons	109

CHAPTER 7

THE ENRICHMENT OF VITAMIN D	114
Check Vitamin D level in children	116
Benefits of vitamin D on children with OI	119
Benefits of vitamin D in dark skinned OI children	121

CHAPTER 8

FAMILY SUPPORT	126
African culture/disability and women	128
My experience	129
Conclusion	133

Testimonials

Dear Reader,

Tarela's latest book, "Unbreakable", Our journey with the brittle bone (OI)condition is fantastic, the book is based on her personal experience and journey! It is easy to read thought-provoking yet, her book takes you through a transformational journey that will give you the confidence to take you to the next level, a huge eye-opener into her world and the reality of OI. As they say, the experience is the best teacher.

Tarela has a true gift to enable ordinary people to live extraordinary lives through releasing themselves from the strongholds and barriers of culture, tradition, and religion; her heart to help people is phenomenal.

Before Tarela, I did not believe that I could achieve great things as I suffer from MS, which affects mostly my muscles. Sometimes my mobility can be poor, making it difficult for me to do certain things for myself, now she has shown me a path to exceptional living and becoming a great person, believing in myself. She is an incredible motivator and an inspiration to us all; her book will take you to new levels in life, which in time will transcend in physical transformation.

Zara-Lucy Whitehead
Beauty Therapist,
Beauty Pageant Queen, UK Model

Dear Reader,

Tarela has written her book Unbreakable" Our journey with brittle bone (OI) condition. The incredible journey she shares with her son, where she has taken you into her world of experience with this rare bone condition which her son is born with, in her book, she has shared her first-hand experience as a mother with a child born with the brittle bone disease in Nigeria, West Africa.

I have personally met this wonderful lady who is very caring and passionate about helping other people living with this rare bone condition as her son. Tarela has shown courage and now supports others suffering from the same condition in Nigeria through the OI charity she foundered in Nigeria (OIF Nigeria).

She works closely with other OI professionals and OI organisation across the African US and UK.

Professor Jean-Marc Retrouvey
Professor and Chair, Department of Orthodontics and Dentofacial Orthopaedics,
Professor in the Department of Orthodontics and Dentofacial Orthopaedics

Provider of quality curriculum development for dental schools and emerging countries.
Craniofacial Research on rare diseases.
Program Director Craniofacial Orthodontics and Director division Orthodontics at McGill University.
President International Foundation for Dental Education.

Dear Reader,

"This book is an eye-opener to the whole new world about this rare disease Osteogenesis Imperfecta (OI), also known as brittle bone disease and Tarela; she genuinely wants you to raise awareness through sharing her experience helping other mums who are going through the same problem to bring change to the oi community and across the globe.

Mrs Mabel Okafor
Winners Chapel, Middlesex.
London, United Kingdom

Dear Reader,

The author Tarela Aghanti has taken me into her amazing walk of life and journey, with a rare bone condition which her son Steven is born with, she has shared her pain, her grief, her fears, her resilience, how she found forgiveness and first-hand experience as mother with a child born with brittle bone (OI) condition.

Tarela Aghanti has shown her courage in the face of her fears and now supporting other parents/ guardian who may be experiencing the same condition in Nigeria and across Africa. She now shares her victory with others, raising brittle bone awareness through her book "Unbreakable".

This book helps you understand the condition of both children and mothers and how communities can also support those families. It is great pleasure to read from our youth Steven who also speaks to the world how his world looks like and how he can compare services that were not available to him in Nigeria and how great his future has shaped up in United Kingdom. Creating improved health and wellness, for persons with OI and improving inclusion and diversity around the world.

-Julliet Makhapila:
London Region Diversity Lead Executive
Community Change Maker, Educator,
Advocate, Social impactor,
Social Scientist, Motivational Speaker,
Fashion model, Host and Presenter,
Entrepreneur and Founder of UK Africa diaspora Forum
@JNM1000

Dear Reader,

The author Tarela Aghanti has taken you into her amazing walk with a rare bone condition, medically known as Osteogenesis Imperfecta aka brittle bone disease, which her son Steven is born with, she has shared her pain, her grief, her fears, and first-hand experience as a mother caring for her son with this disease.

I have known Tarela Aghanti for a while now, who is passionate about raising oi awareness and supporting others with oi and other physically challenged persons.
She is resilient... proven "unbreakable" in her pain and suffering that she has passed through over the years, she has shown her bravery and continuous courage in the face of her fears and now supporting others suffering from the same condition in Nigeria, Africa, and the UK where she resides.

With this book, she shares her experiences with you, raising brittle bone (OI) awareness "Unbreakable".

Prof. Abiola Oduwole

Professor of Paediatrics and Paediatric Endocrinology

College of Medicine, University of Lagos

Chief Coordinator, Paediatric Endocrinology Training Centre for West Africa

Lagos University Teaching Hospital (LUTH)

Dear Reader

Tarela has gone all the way supporting and confidently motivating people anywhere she goes. I never believe that I could achieve things as I suffer from brittle bone myself and a member of the osteogenesis Imperfecta foundation which is founded by Tarela Aghanti to support people suffering from brittle bone disease. This condition affects mostly my bones and muscles and mobility which makes it so difficult for me to walk without an aid.

Sometimes my mobility very poor, making it difficult for me to do certain things for myself so I strongly depend on my family for support, now she has shown me a path to exceptional living and becoming a great person through her support and oi conferences held through the years.

Tarela has thought me to believe in myself. She is an incredible motivator and an inspiration to us all with a great personality; her book will take you to new levels in life, which in time will transform you.

Blessing G. Nweze

Member OIF Nigeria (OIFN)

Dear Reader,

Tarela Aghanti is the mother of Steven, a young adult living with Osteogenesis Imperfecta, a rare bone condition which causes the bones to break easily and numerous other challenges. Since Steven was born, she has shared everything he was going through: his pain and joy, his fear and his hopes, his frustrations and his progress working hard to achieve a good quality of life. In this book Tarela Aghanti has shown her courage in the face of her fears. She now is now supporting others who have the same condition in Nigeria and many other places in the world. Her new book "Unbreakable" will help to raise awareness for brittle bones disease. An inspiring read for everyone living based on faith, love, and hope.

Dagmar Mekking

Founder and Chairperson

Foundation Care4BrittleBones

FOREWORD

Tarela has a unique individual and has an amazing personality, enabling ordinary people to live extraordinary lives by releasing themselves from the strongholds of pain and trauma. Her heart to help people is Phenomenal and her strong faith in God inspires her to care for others showing God's heart to people. Tarela has set up Osteogenesis Imperfecta Foundation (Nigeria) and Osteogenesis Imperfecta Foundation Network (UK), which aims to supports Children and Families Living with Brittle bone (OI) diseases to give them improved Life opportunities. Her active partnership with various stakeholders creates OI awareness in Nigeria and across Africa. Tarela aims to show you how she can live an exceptional life even in the face of this rear condition with her son, believing more in self that "I can do it, and staying positive. She is an incredible advocate, international speaker, and inspiration to us all. Buying this book will also support ongoing works of (OI Foundations) visions and gives you a chance of reflecting upon your journey. It also allows you to help a family living with disabilities. Start today to find out what unbreakable is.

Mrs I.O Oshodi
Member of the Board of Trustees
Foundation for promotion of Child Care Development
FPCD
Deputy South West Zonal Coordinator (CSCSD)
National President/Executive Director
Association for Childhood Education Practitioners
(ACEP)
National Council of Child Rights Advocate of Nigeria, an organization with Special Consultative status with UN.

APPRECIATION

I acknowledge God Almighty for keeping me safe, for being the backbone in this journey of my life and placing me at a place of rest, giving me the ability and courage to write this book. I acknowledge you for receiving this book and using it in the most positive way that you know.

To my loving husband Victor Aghanti, for his unwavering support, his encouragement has been very instrumental in my ability for all my work to serve and support others, to communicate to the world my experience and our life journey with the brittle bone disease (OI). To my children, Daniel, Steven, and Valerie thank you all for your understanding, your patience, and steadfast love.

My profound gratitude to an Amazon, Mrs. Jere Ehirebe, a solicitor in UK and Nigeria, for all her support during my dark days; she was my strength; I remember the very first day we met in her office with my son Steven, she was compassionate on my situation and decided to take a very bold and brave step in helping us in the best way possible. When I look back at all she has done for me today, I cannot but smile and be so lost in gratitude to her. She stood by me, helped me stand strong, and push me on with her kind words of encouragement and prayers.

Bethany Community Church has always been a significant source of a support network for me, both spiritually and physically, interested in our total wellbeing; they have always supported the less privileged both locally, nationally, and globally and have supported myself and my family in numerous ways especially in our life journey for which I am most grateful.

Bethany is not just a modern-day church but a complete practical demonstration of God's heart. Bethany has worked with people without discrimination or being judgmental and has supported OI children and their families in Nigeria through the OIFN; what a remarkable way they have shown God's amazing love?

And lastly, my profound appreciation is to Maureen Whitehead, for being a wonderful sister walking along with me on this road of a life-changing experience. Maureen tirelessly worked so hard to fundraise for Steven's operations, determined to see him have adequate medical help and for standing by me all through, she is a wonderful sister and a real gem.

Note to the Reader

All information, including opinions and analyses, is based on the author's personal experiences and is not intended to provide professional advice. The author and the publisher make no warranties, either expressed or implied, concerning the accuracy, applicability, effectiveness, reliability, or suitability of the contents. If you wish to apply or follow the advice or recommendations mentioned herein, you take full responsibility for your actions. The author and publisher of this book shall in no event be held liable for any direct, indirect, incidental, or consequential damages arising directly or indirectly from the use of any of the information contained in this book.

All content is for information only and is not warranted for content accuracy or any other implied or explicit purposes.

CHAPTER 1

LIVING WITH BRITTLE BONE (OI) DISEASE

CHAPTER 1
LIVING WITH BRITTLE BONE (OI) DISEASE

In this chapter, I need to explain to you in full details and simple language what is Osteogenesis Imperfecta (OI), also known as brittle bone disease, to help you have a better understanding as we carry on.

Osteogenesis imperfecta (OI) is a genetic disorder that prevents the body from building strong bones. People with OI might have bones that break easily, so the condition is commonly called brittle bone disease; this bone disease is passed down through families and can also be inherited. It is caused by a defect in a gene that is supposed to make a substance called collagen. Collagen is a protein in your body that forms and strengthens bones during the fetus's development in the womb during pregnancy.

People have struggled so much with this word disease, it makes it sound infectious like the next person standing or sitting beside you can catch brittle bone but that is not the case, far from the truth, brittle bone is not an infection which makes it impossible for anyone to catch, it is a genetic condition, meaning, it is in the gene from birth, that is why I prefer to use the word condition instead of disease.

There are at least 19 recognized forms of osteogenesis imperfecta, designated type I through type XIX. Several types are distinguished by their signs and symptoms, although their characteristic features overlap. Increasingly, genetic causes are used to define rarer forms of osteogenesis imperfecta. The disease is divided into eight different types designated by the Roman numerals I through VIII. The kind of disease of the bone is determined by the particular genetic mutation and pattern of inheritance, which can vary from mild to serve where service can break any part of the bone as many times as possible due to the bone's fragility.

What Are the Types of Brittle Bone Disease?

Type 1 OI. Type 1 OI is the mildest and most common form of brittle bone disease. ...

Type 2 OI. Type 2 OI is the most severe form of brittle bone disease, and it can be life-threatening. ...

Type 3 OI. Type 3 OI is also a severe form of brittle bone disease. ...

Type 4 OI. Osteogenesis imperfecta type IV is a moderate kind of osteogenesis imperfecta (OI; see this term). It is a genetic disorder characterized by increased bone fragility, low bone mass, and bone fracture susceptibility.

My son Steven was diagnosed with OI type III serve, he had constant fractures and have broken every part of his body that you can think of, sometimes he can have multiple fractures simultaneously, till date Steven has had over a hundred fracture that we have stopped counting, he has undergone four major corrective rodding surgeries on both legs, and he is still having zoledronic acid which I call bone juice to help strengthen his bones.

The only way I can describe living with the brittle bone condition in Nigeria was like living in HELL. If I must be honest, this was due to a lot of factors which I would list as I go along in this book, I am sure you can also tell or imagine some of it already.

There are severe forms of this disease that can also affect the rib cage and spine's shape, leading to life-threatening breathing problems. Some people may need to be placed on oxygen. Still, in many other cases, people living with this condition can live a healthy, productive life with proper maintenance, regular monitoring, and the right treatment in place, especially when the child is diagnosed early enough. In our case, Steven was not diagnosed until he was three years of age in the UK at the Great Ormond Hospital under Dr. Roposh, who is a wonderful doctor. Before he got diagnosed, we were living in Nigeria without any form of knowledge on the condition and what we were dealing with was hell in every form of it. We could not find another person with the same problem or diagnosis as the brittle bone disease is an exceedingly rare condition worldwide and even more rare in Nigeria, with all the beliefs I will describe in my upcoming chapters. Lack of knowledge was a significant problem that led to mismanagement, miss handling; Religious jargon did not help either; again, ignorance played a huge part that I can boldly say "ignorance is a disease" and its cost is huge.

My son has fractured every bone you can think of on his body from head to toe, over a hundred fractures and four major corrective rodding surgeries on both legs, and the effect of constant fracture has taken its toll on his body making some part of his body deformed which is another issue that we had to deal with mentally, emotionally, and physically. He is a warrior and a survivor. Steven was diagnosed with type three serve OI, one of the worst forms of brittle bone disease. (again, I hate to use the word disease because it makes the condition sound infectious, which is not.

Now that he is in his teens, he receives care under doctor Benjamin Jacobs for Zoledronic Acid and Doctor Calder, his surgeon at RNOH Stanmore UK. Receiving this innovative quality care from orthopaedic specialists has made Life a lot easier, stable and has helped Steven live Life like any other teenage boy, which has allowed me time, space, and the passion to starting up Osteogenesis Imperfecta foundation Nigeria (OIFN) and now Osteogenesis Imperfecta Foundation Network UK to raise awareness to support children and families living with the brittle bone condition in the UK, Nigeria, and Africa as a whole, so parents and their children don't have to go through what I went through in my darkest days in silence. My mission is to give them a hand to hold on to, walk through their OI journey, raise awareness at the grassroots level, and more, medical professionals in our world, etc.

Our experience and journey with this condition have made us stronger together as a family. Unfortunately, it may have broken others with each family member gone their separate ways; fortunately for us, it brought us together, totally dependent on each other as a family unit and God the father. I will be sincere here, it has not been easy, but this has made me know that we can always scale through victoriously in any circumstance we find ourselves giving the right tool and the right help and with God placed as our centrepiece. (For with God, nothing is impossible). Luke 1:37 & Luke 18:27 & Matt 19:26.

It has taken me over ten years to finally get to this comfortable and confident place to be able to put this book together to share my experience, of shame, my pain, trauma, agony, and relief which in a way is exciting. The journey has not been easy as I mentioned earlier, but it has all come together. All thanks and glory to my father God in heaven for his grace, guidance, and unfailing love that has propelled me through tough times to a pedal of safety, and now I can say humbly I am unbrokenly standing strong and tall.

Sometimes we find ourselves in a situation beyond us that sets in confusion, pain, anxiety, and depression, we tend to want to quit, but I must say to you, it is not the time to give up and allow the situation or circumstance you find yourself to consume you. At this point you need to stop and think, there must be a way out, as giving up is not an option because the problem you are going through can only refine you into a better person if you do not give up and quit.

Situations in life can either make you or break you, but the good news is that you have the power of choice, you can choose either one.... make you? Or break you? Choose one. If you do not quit, you can later in life help others coming behind that find themselves in the situation you found yourself because you have gained the experience needed and become well known to help them, remember, things happen for a reason, you need to stop and ask yourself WHY? WHAT?... The quicker you learn the lesson that needs learning and figure things out, the quicker you move on.

In all my pain, trouble, agony, and trauma, in the end, it all turned out that I can use my experience to support, advise, educate, befriend, and coach others and their families, helping them find strength, peace, and accepting their situation and their disability, which is fulfilling.

Psalms 59:16 GNB

"But I will sing about your strength; every morning I will sing aloud of your constant love. You have been a refuge for me, a shelter in my time of trouble".

CHAPTER 2

Facing your fear

CHAPTER 2

Facing your fear

Fear is an unpleasant emotion caused by the threat of danger, pain, or harm, even trauma, it keeps you bound feeling insecure. Most of us are scared and worry a lot, and most suffer from anxiety and guilt, which many mothers and carers with children with different disabilities including

OI experience. People often blame themselves for having a child with a disability. Some people blame others as they face stigmatization in the society, some people blame themselves and take responsibility for their kids' physical, mental outcome; the society and their extended family in most cases do not help as they centre it all to your fault, this is mostly experienced in the black community.

I was blessed to have a very understanding and supportive family that went all the way in reaching out to me whenever I needed help, and this made a huge positive difference in my life, and that also made life bearable in the circumstances I find myself.

Facing my fears was very scary and unpleasant, and at the same time, I knew it was something I had to do if I had to move forward in life. I was always afraid of my son having another fracture, the trauma of facing another break was devastating and demoralising. I could not tell if I had the inner strength to handle it, but that did not stop the fractures from happening; I realized that at any time it happens, I had to deal with it without thinking twice about it or hesitating to give care, LOVE, needed attention to my frail child every time we went through a new chapter of breaks in our lives, even though very stressful.

I think it is important to give a good scenario of when we attend to a breaking while back in Nigeria.

We had no car of our own; and live far from the bus stop, we will have to walk quite a distance from our house to get to the bus stop to board the bus to the hospital with all eye on you starring, people wondering and saying "NOT AGAIN" sometimes you can hear them talk and sometimes you can just feel it. On reaching the hospital, after seeing the doctor then we get referred for an ex-ray, from the hospital to the location for the ex-ray was another distance, after the ex-ray, we will have to make another trip by bus back to the hospital for stabilization and pain meds to help reduce the level of pain and calm his temperature down after that have plaster put on him. Sometimes it might be just a fracture, and sometimes it might be multiple fractures on different parts of his body which means the plaster is on all affected areas of his body. I remember a few times where he had plastered on both legs and one hand at the same time.

This period can be very traumatizing and stressful; he was always in constant pain, unlike the western world where the child is placed on morphine and closely monitored by the pain management team to help manage the unbearable pain he was having. I remember him going for several days and weeks crying due to the excruciating pain he was having, and I could do nothing to help or stop the pain nor the cry.

Steven was not able to attend school as no school in my area where we lived would admit him after telling them his history of fracture as the schools had no experience on the condition nor heard about brittle bone (OI), they did not want to take the risk and responsibility, so at age three my darling son had no form of education which was something that bordered me a lot. Now with an awareness campaign on brittle bone condition through OIF Nigeria, things are beginning to change for good as some schools are beginning to admit children with this condition, supporting them with early childhood learning because we believe no child should be left behind in education irrespective of their ability or disability.

Putting all these down in writing just brings back all the painful memories. I can feel my chest pounding, my eyes whaling up, and tears rolling down my cheek. It is a place where I pray no one should be, not even my enemy, a pain no one should experience, trust me, it is excruciatingly painful- you have no idea, I have no word to describe how excruciatingly painful it was, the fact that I couldn't take that pain away from him and help my darling son at that moment killed me over and over again, deep inside I was so helpless, confused and completely broken as all I could do was cry with him and watched him cry.... trust me those were my days of thick darkness. For several years I was captured by all these thoughts and trauma, and I must confess it did bring me a great deal of fear, kept me from reaching out and moving on.

Some people might differ, feeling guilty for having that condition, which can lead to so many problems like isolating themselves, feeling insecure, which can lead to an inferiority complex, thereof.

Sometimes fear can be beneficial, it keeps us from harm, but many times, it is an inner voice of fear and sometimes guilt and barrier that keeps us stuck for a very long time; it keeps us from getting what we want, reaching our goal and becoming who we want to be in Life. Learning to handle fear and overcoming fear is essential – even if sometimes you would love to experience not being afraid for just a few moments or few days so you can take a meaningful action…. then it is worth it – it -is critical for living your full potential in life. If you are struggling with fear or anxiety, I would love to recommend a few tips to help you move on. These are tips that I have personally used, and they worked for me, hence I am confidently recommending them, so maybe you could also try them for yourself.

Feel free to talk about it:

When it comes to the past, silence can be deadly, and it is extremely helpful to stop pretending and free yourself from the bondage of holding it all in, talking about what is tearing you apart inside. Express the emotions you feel inside to a counselor, mentor, or friend you can trust. healing starts with being honest and vulnerable about who you are…the good and the bad, so it is worth saying all you need to say, it does help.

Be truthful with yourself:

We tend to think; maybe it will all go away if we pretend it never happened, that is far from the truth; we must choose to break out of denial and self-pity. Be honest about your situation—Journal out the specifics causing you pain and anger. As humans, we are bound to make mistakes in life so let us face the facts here. You will hurt people sometimes, you will have regrets, it is all part of living in an imperfect world, but remember, you have a choice, it's either your past will keep you in a rut of fear, shame, and guilt... or you will accept it for what it is, experience the freedom of moving on and enjoy the now as life is too short to live it all in self-denial and fear, understanding that self-acceptance is critical to your emotional health and total well-being is very important, so do not miss out on that!

Self-Love /Acceptance:

One of the ways I could conquer my fear was by accepting the situation and the condition my child has and trust in God for improvement, better health, and living. Accepting your child with a disability is one thing and accepting your situation is another. I had to take a little review for myself, and I knew I did nothing wrong even when society may have me think otherwise; I had to way up to everything, find a way to find my inner peace trusting in God, at that point, something broke inside of me, I came to realize that I had to come to a place of acceptance of my child's condition even though I accepted my child as my child, immediately that happened inside of me, things turned around and life became much easier.

If you are feeling guilty for having passed the problem or condition unto your child, this is the point where you need to free yourself from that and show yourself some self-love to help you move on. Self-love is inherent in every one of us and necessary for living a wholesome life. On the other hand: Is there a form of unhealthy self-love that breeds selfishness and arrogance? And how is that different from healthy self-love that fosters self-esteem and self-confidence? But remember, it is essential to create a positive balance between humility, self-love, and selflessness. It is also necessary to know that you cannot love others or your child with a disability without first loving yourself .... "you cannot give what you don't have". "Accept what you cannot change". Accept who you are and leave the rest to God. Change needs to happen for your benefit.... It is how you see yourself or your child that matters. Do not worry about how society or others see you or your child or what people will say. If you love and accept yourself; if you love your child with a disability, others will follow suit as it all needs to starts with "YOU."

Even though my friends despised my son because of his condition, they made negative comments and laughed, and made worse acts than I can imagine, I still loved him.

I remember taking Steven for an ex-ray after another break, on reaching the lab, one of the staff was very ready to beat me up, claiming he has seen me with my son there on several occasions for the same complaint of fracture, the ex-ray has confirmed fractured bones, this occasion, the staff felt I was intentionally causing injury on him and felt I was a terrible mother. He rolled up his sleeves and trousers, took off his shoes, raised his hand ready to lay them on me. It was incredibly shocking how people who do not even know you or your circumstance or history draw their conclusions and cause you more trauma by laying hands on you, even thinking to do so was bad enough.

Food for thought:

"If they have not tied to break me, I would never know that I am unbreakable".

Forgive yourself:

I cannot over-emphasis this subject of forgiveness; I have already written a book on forgiveness titled "FORGIVENESS IS KEY" Your Inner secret To A Healthy Life. You cannot talk about disability and not touch on forgiveness as this is one major issue that affects so many of us and has completely crumbled people living with different kinds of disability including brittle bone. I will encourage you to get this book on Amazon or through my website www.tarelaaghanti.com.

I will only speak a little on this subject here. Forgiveness is an extraordinarily strong and powerful tool; let us quickly look at forgiveness as I believe understanding the word forgiveness will help you have a deeper understanding of its importance as it helped transform my life. Forgiveness is the intentional and voluntary process by which a person undergoes a change in feelings and attitude regarding an offense and overcoming negative emotions such as resentment and vengeance, bitterness, anger, regret, trauma, and pain from their past;

however, justified their actions might be. As a Christian myself, the Bible talks a lot about forgiveness as a tool to help us move on in life. Forgiveness itself is very important for your mental health and stability. By so practicing forgiveness, you can wave off the root and causes of so many illnesses.

Being afraid of the unknown, things you do not have control over can be so worrying and demoralizing; it can completely paralyze you from head to toe, as it happened in my case – not having a clue or knowledge on this condition that my son had, why he broke bones, why he could not sit nor walk or even develop as his peers did. It can also stop you from letting go or achieving your goal and purpose in life, which I did fully experienced, but it all changed when I truly understood forgiveness and consciously made a commitment for change by letting go.

For some people, forgiving others or even themselves is a huge problem. The fact that they have a child with a disability is extremely difficult for them to deal with and that can become noticeable in all their dealing with the child, especially if they live in a community or culture that always fault them for that, so they carry the burden of self-guilt on their shoulders for a very long time which can be a very heavyweight to bear.

Let the past be past. It is good to live in the present so I would encourage you to stop beating yourself up about something that happened years ago, consciously banish and reject guilt and shame from controlling your thoughts and behaviors. It is important not to hold on to those guilt as it can destroy you inside which will reflect outwardly too. You do not need to justify your past action or try to prove yourself to anyone, letting go of the past means burying it and giving up your right to engage in self-condemnation, but permitting yourself to breathe the fresh air and live-in freedom. You need to understand that Forgiveness is a choice, also a process. It is a deliberate and consciously choosing to stop blaming and hating yourself or putting yourself down. Instead, see yourself as a valuable human being with great potentials, full of ideas to contribute to this world for growth.

· One of the first steps of letting go is believing in yourself that you can do It; secondly, get it all out. You can also speak to someone or a counselor to help you pass the stage where you are.

Praying about it and asking people you trust to pray with you also help as I strongly believe that prayer is a powerful tool that has helped me in my journey too. I remember so many times after a break, all I could do was cry as I was completely shattered and, in a wreck, could not find the strength to speak nor pray. Those were times and days I relied on my family for their hugs, comfort, and covering of prayers over me.

Accept yourself as you are and accept the fact, situation, and reality that faces you-do not be in denial, it is so dangerous to live in self-denial.

"For sure this world breaks everyone, afterward, some are stronger at their broken places, remember strength does not come from winning, but your struggles develop your strengths, every time you go through hardships and decide not to surrender, that, I say is STRENGTH.

In my observation through life experiences, I believe there are two ways of exerting one's strength: one is pushing up, the other is pulling down; after all, In a race, there might be better starters than yourself but remember you can be a stronger finisher and you can pick up momentum at the middle of the race to push you through to the end for a stronger and better finish, it's not how you start the race that matters, but it's how much continuous effort and struggle you put in to get you to your finish line, therefore, it is paramount to encourage you to make up your mind today that no matter what comes your way, no matter how difficult it gets, no matter how unfair the world maybe or the situation you find yourself may get you down, do more than simply survive.

You will thrive despite what... Just remember this, tough times never last, but tough people do, and you can do all things through Christ who strengthens you.

I put God as my centrepiece; I believe I am strong in him when everything seems to be going wrong. I think that tomorrow is another day, and my tomorrow will be better than my today as I am dependable on God's power with full assurance that he is always with me and can take me through thick and thin, to safety and dryer grounds. So have FAITH, keep STRONG and stay FOCUSED". (Keep your eyes fixed on positivity through God) for your better tomorrow.

CHAPTER 3

Springing forth with a child with OI/disability

CHAPTER 3
Springing forth with a child with OI/disability

Disability itself can crumble one as a person. According to research, one billion people around the world live with some form of disability, making up around 15% of the global population. The vast majority of people living with disabilities live in developing countries.

According to the World Report on Disability, the number of people with disabilities is increasing by the day due to so many factors which I will not go into here but despite being "despite the increasing number", people with disabilities are often forgotten. They regularly face discrimination and exclusion from water and sanitation, healthcare, education, work, and community life. And even though disabled people are among the poorest and most vulnerable, their needs are often overlooked by governments and by international organisations which in my opinion needs to change, however, efforts to bring about change and improve life can only be effective if we raise awareness, include people with living with brittle bone disease and other disabilities!

People living with a disability, their careers, family members have gone through so many struggles, isolation, neglect, hate, and much more which have made them lose hope and felt forgotten and let down by their society and all of these have their effect of individuals living with a disability. But in all of these, if we find ourselves dwelling in these negativities, we will never move on which again is where living freely through letting go and forgiveness comes in. I have come to realise that there is no way one can talk about disability with all the pain it brings that you cannot touch on forgiveness if you must move from the place of pain and rot people with disability find themselves, just like I did.

Forgiveness, acceptance, and self-love must be deeply investigated and well understood as a mother with a child with a disability. Accepting your fate, accepting that child is one and accepting the child with the condition is another. Most people will have to come to terms with the fact that they have a child with a disability and move on, it does not either is it healthy nor does it help the mind, soul, and body to constantly self-blame even if the world we find ourselves say otherwise.

Forgiving yourself— "Self-Love" It is incredibly important to practice some self-love by forgiving yourself even though I understand that it can also be one of the most difficult things to do in life. It takes true strength to forgive yourself for the wrong that you have done in the past or to forgive someone who has hurt you badly in the past and never cared to apologize. Forgiving yourself for having a child with a disability might sometimes be very difficult for some, knowing that you or your child is never accepted by your family or the society at large. I have had to forgive others who never apologized for wronging and despised my child, and I have had to forgive myself for many shameful and regretful actions that I have committed.

Jesus himself knew this, that is why he preaches and encourages us to forgive. Jesus understands that it is the key to freedom, whether it be your spiritual or physical life, both can change and flourish through practicing forgiveness. Once I did, the weight was lifted off me and my heart became burden-free. The following Bible verses helped me when my heart was so better, and I hope they also help you who is struggling to forgive.

Your peace:

Even though you feel that they do not deserve it because of the depth of the hurt they have caused you, and even if you feel you do not have to. One thing I want you to always keep at the back of your mind is that in this case, it is all about you having and living in peace so understand that you are doing it for "YOU" and for no one else.

We all at some point offend or hurt someone, whether it is done knowingly or unknowingly. We all hurt someone at some point in our life, so in the same way that you expect them to forgive you when you hurt them, so, likewise, you also need to forgive others when they hurt or offend you. In my world, I have realised that forgiving each other makes the world a better place to live in. When you hold onto resentment towards another, you are bound to that person or condition by an emotional link that is stronger than anything else. Forgiveness is the only way to break that link and to gain your freedom, although, as I said earlier, forgiveness does not change the past, it does enlarge the future and is the key to living a healthy life. If you are contemplating how to forgive someone, I believe it may help you if you express your feelings and hurt to the other person as that will help clear the air. If the relationship is important to you and you would like to continue with it, it may be useful for you to tell the other person how their actions affected you. If the person is no longer in your life, if you want to cut off the relationship, or if you have reason to believe that things will get much worse if you directly address the situation, you may want to just write a letter stating the incident, expressing your hurt, and pouring out how and what you are feeling does help. This can help but remember to tear up the letter or better still, burn it and move on. It may help to put your feelings into words as part of letting go and your healing process.

A lot of times people have asked me, do I need to let the other person know that I have forgiven them? In my opinion, there is no need to let them know that you have forgiven them if you do not feel comfortable approaching them especially if they have not personally come to you directly acknowledging their fault in the situation and asking for your forgiveness.

Forgiveness is very important to help reduce anger in you and your child who have suffered like in my case, it helped me with a stable and meaningful relationship with others without anger causing discord and division wherever I found myself in my community or among the people who have hurt me and caused me trauma in the past.

There are a lot of benefits to why you must forgive whether be it yourself or others that have offended you, called your names, or even your child and I will advise you to take this very seriously because it has the potentials to help you unlock yourself from the trauma or pain thereby accepting yourself, it will help you walk away from self-denial and accepting your child as they are and above all moving on, resulting to living freely, honestly there no amount of money that can buy the joy that comes with that deep feeling of living in total freedom-it is priceless.

- It can help Improved mental health: This is a big issue that many people suffer from unforgiveness, to shock you, this has been proven scientifically.
- Strengthens your immune system
- Improves self-esteem
- Lowers the risk of high blood pressure and hypertension
- Helps you with a healthy lifestyle
- Extremely healthy relationships with others.
- Improves the health of your heart.

Feeling Worthless and Shame:

Having a disability, yourself, or caring for a child with a disability in the African setting can bring with it lots of shame and guilt, these feelings can lead so many parents and carers into suffering depression. Guilt is associated with wrongdoing, an activity, which tends to leave a person feeling uncomfortable while shame is a deep inner experience of being "not wanted". It is feeling worthless, rejected, cast out and these two go together.

Shame always carries with it the sense that there is nothing you can do to purge its burdensome and toxic presence. Carrying shaming with you is so weakening making you feel so worthless and insignificant that you develop ways both conscious and unconscious isolate yourself. Some people sometimes strongly feel the humiliation, feeling worthless, embarrassed, and above all, powerless to get rid of the shame because of something from their past. Do you know that with some people it might not stop there, if you cannot get rid of these terrible feelings, do away with the burden of that shame and guilt that you carry, there is every possibility that it can worsen into rejection because you feel you are not good enough and nobody wants you? It is also proven that where there is depression, there is usually rejection. The need for love, acceptance, and self-worth is one of the strongest basic human needs, depression from rejection attaches itself to that part of our nature which desires love and acceptance and the need for self-worth.

For you to have a fulfilling life, you need to go back to the basics, so you can be free from depression and rejection because these can be replaced with peace and joy.

Need for acceptance. Need to feel loved. Need not be alone. Need to be in the in-crowd! Need to have listened too! Need for significance! The feeling of Condemnation Feeling unworthy. Guilt, shame from disability,

As you can see all these can be linked together, just because you have and care for a child with a disability means you have a lot to lose if you decide to carry on in self-denial and forgiveness towards yourself and others, at the end of the day it is you and you alone that losses everything, no one else.

Regret, unwanted feeling:

This is a terrible and deep feeling of sadness or disappointment over having a child with such a condition hmmm, you need to be very careful so as not to be consumed with issues that can come with regret and guilt, and shame as it can be detrimental to you in so many ways. So many people walk around carrying so much guilt and regret with them, either from past incidents and having a child with a disability, past mistakes, an accident that turned into a life-limiting illness, or having a disability, all this can cause trauma, guilt, and regret wishing you would have done things differently, this may lead to irritation, which can cause lots of tension within, then progress to guilt and regrets. If you do not let, go of the guilt, and regrets it can rein you in so many ways which at this point I will recommend you speak to someone for help.

Communicating this to someone can help reduce the tension you are carrying, to talk about how you are coping with what the situation may be can also help you understand it and can result in having solutions. No matter what happens, remember forgiveness in every form of it is all about "YOU" and no one else. It is about having your peace, your health, and your child's. Personally, I realised this the very hard way and when I did, I was so glad, and I have never regretted it or looked back or wished for anything else. It pays to be FREE, even though I still care for my son with brittle bone condition, it makes no difference to me now because we are all disabled and able in one way or another.

No Regrets….. Freedom all the way…..

CHAPTER 4

Tradition and culture

CHAPTER 4

Tradition and culture

Without going too deep into the definitions of both terms, I can tell you that tradition is used to describe beliefs and behaviors that are passed on from generation to generation, while culture is used to describe the characteristics of a certain society at a particular point in time and these two go hand in hand. With around 250 ethnic groups, Nigeria has an extensive list of traditions and customs that Nigerians live by. While a majority of these cultures and traditions are similar to those from other parts of the world, here are some unique traditions and customs that Nigerians, Asian, and other African countries are known for, but to write this book, I will strictly stick to a very few that are relevant to my book.

These cultures can be very rich in their own rights; it feels exciting when present at the display of these traditions during ceremonies, but hopefully, you will understand it as I would do my best to carry you along to help you understand how deep these traditions and cultures are practiced.

Different stages of weddings:

Nigerians and Africans are expected to have three different stages of wedding ceremonies. The first one is the introduction/traditional wedding. Depending on what part of the country you are from, formally introducing the husband to be. These involve the bride being escorted out by her sister, her friends, generally by the ladies in her household with great singing, dancing, all dressed up, sometimes with heavily beaded jewelry, traditional fancy native dresses with the most amazing headgears, brides price, mass prostrations by the groom to be and his men entourage, palm wine carrying, picking out your spouse from a line of thoroughly veiled women or the lady picking out her husband to be from the line of seated men, the bride will have to identify her groom to be with a native calabash cup of palm wine, followed with prayers offered by both parents of the bride and groom to be.

After which comes to the court and church/mosque weddings, in this way, a couple's union has been legally recognized by the provisions of African traditions, cultures, religion, and civil law, and to say that all three weddings also involve feasting, therefore, the couple needs to be financially prepared for this as well.

These cultures and traditions are rich with flamboyant dressing, it can be beautiful and elaborate, but under any circumstances or reasons the couple comes together without these rites being carried out or performed by the groom to be and his family and death occur, maybe the woman dies, the ceremony MUST be done before the woman's body is laid to mother earth. This gives you a good background and understanding of how deep, strong, and meaningful tradition and culture are and how seriously they are taken.

Pre-Marital Introduction Ceremonies:

No matter how long you have been courting your partner, the relationship remains unrecognized until the formal introduction ceremony. However, this also means the couple is ready to tie the knot. Traditionally, the introduction ceremony takes place in the bride-to-be's family home. Her spouse's people come to the house to pay their respects to her family to "state their intentions" for marriage asking the lady's hand in marriage. After the bride-to-be's family accepts the official proposal, both families share food and drinks. These days, however, introduction ceremonies are as good as one of the three wedding ceremonies that most African and Asian communities usually observe. After these stages, they can have a white wedding if they wish to. If not, they can decide to have a court wedding to sign their wedding certificate to officially legalize their marriage vows.

After-Birth Care:

Extremely significant among the African culture and tradition, this is also widely practiced across Nigerian tribes and other African countries. It is known as "omugwo." The Yorubas call it "Itoju omo," Igalas call it "Iwagwala-oma," and the Annangs, after a mother gives birth to her baby, her mother-in-law, or the bride's mothers comes to the home to take care of the new mother and the new-born. The nursing mother is not required to lift a finger as everything is done for her—including bathing the baby, and massaging the new-born baby, performing household chores, cooking special meals such as pepper soups, and much more. If a mother-in-law is unavailable for an omugwo, the woman's aunt or a close female relative can take up that role. Omugwo is a thing of pride and so symbolic that they have been known to cause quarrels among family members who are most capable of caring for the nursing mother and her new baby. Omugwos last for at least three months.

In the western world, these practices of "After Birth care" might be done but not as deep as the other cultural heritage backgrounds. The western also carries out baby massage to enhance the baby's bowel movement and promote bonding of both mother and child.

Tradition and culture shape the way people perceive life and situations in life, which can be in their extremities and can be detrimental in most cases, especially to babies with the brittle bone condition. Although these countries can be affluent in the display of their beautiful cultural heritage and traditions, at the same time, the same beautiful, rich traditions and culture can quickly become ugly and cruel when it comes to families and children living with one form of disability including brittle bone condition.

To top it all up, the extremities of these religions, traditions, and culture have superstitious beliefs that have compounded the problem of people living with disabilities in many communities across the globe. Many families have been demonized, helpless.... stereotyped, treated as outcasts, and ostracized, unloved and despised, labeled in different forms, called names associated with ancestral curses and sin even dehumanized in worse cases. I will touch more on these in chapter five.

— People with disabilities may be presumed to be helpless, unable to care for themselves, unable to make their own decisions, unable to have emotions, love, or be loved. We need to understand that all these factors affect people living with disability in different aspects and level of life, stigma can be associated with mental illness which affects their overall wellbeing, therefore, has to be considered very carefully.

CHAPTER 5

Grandma Care and treatment "Massage at bath time."

CHAPTER 5
Grandma Care and treatment "Massage at bath time."

The rich, long-standing tradition in African communities whereby a new-born child is being massaged during bath time, contradicts the safe handling of an infant with brittle bone (OI) condition. The solution is needed to foster infants' safe handling, we understand that grandma care treatment has been from time immemorial; it is a practice that has been from the time of our forefathers and is well-practiced in a lot of the African countries, including countries like Asia, the Chinese, this practice is spreading fast across the globe, which is also, now practiced in the western world by a professional baby masseuse.

In the past, it is believed that this practice or care provided by grandmas have been of great help and advantage to children in general but research and recent development of broader knowledge and from my personal experience have proven that such treatment is not suitable for children with the brittle bone (OI) condition as brittle bone disease or condition is the defect of collagen in an affected person, therefore, causing fragility of the bone, making it prone to fractures. Due to the fragility of the bone, this type of treatment is not advisable for infants, toddlers, and Adolescents with the brittle bone (OI) because of the long-term damage and trauma associated with such treatment; it is also important to stress the psychological damage it has on the parents cannot be overemphasized and should not be overlooked.

What is Grandma care or grandma's treatment?

I have defined this type of care /treatment as the care provided by a woman who has made herself available and taken up the responsibility to take care of a new-born after birth to give respite, saving the mother of the child enough rest time to help recover from childbirth. In (Nigeria, Africa), it is popularly known as (omugwo), just as I have explained in chapter 2 above.

In Nigeria, grandmothers are traditionally involved in the care of new-borns, and they often play the role of a midwife.

In the first few weeks of the baby's life, grandmothers assist with the bathing of the child, aiding the healing process of the umbilical cord which is crucial, and carefully done with the use of native ointment and heat to aid quick healing.

- Bathing and massage treatment of the baby's body often involves twisting of the hands backward, legs forward, and backward to achieve flexibility, but the real question here is it true and helpful?
- Holding them upside down.
- Shake them around and throwing them upward to remove the fear of height.
- Twisting of the baby's little hands (gently) behind reaching the baby's shoulder blades.
- Bending the knees until the heel touches the baby's bottom.
- Pressing and massaging the baby's stomach down with warm water with the use of a small face towel.
- Massage of the baby's head to help shape up and properly molded, giving it a round circular shape as they grow.
- Vigorous massaging of the baby's legs, arms, back, bottom, chest, and stomach, etc....

While we are not necessarily told why this is done, with time I carried out a little research of mine and it appears the reason this is done is to relax the babies nerves and muscles because it is believed that the baby has been curled up in the mother's womb for nine months, therefore, these type of treatment will straighten the babies nerves and also strengthen the baby's muscles which allow for more flexible and ease bowel movement.

This type of massage is done with the application of intense pressure, which is absolutely not necessary, not appropriate, and damaging to children with brittle bone conditions.

Sometimes feeding is often done forcefully whereby the baby is laid flat on the grandmother's lap and sometimes tilted upside-down almost 60-degree angle with the nostrils of the child closed with two figures of the grandma to force and fasten the swallowing of the liquid food down the child but this act can only be carried out on children from 7+ months old if they the child is refusing food, which, again, I personally do not approve off. As the baby grows, a crawling child could be strapped to a fixed object like a chair to limit mobility. Circumcision is also a rite for the male in most African cultural communities and females in a few ethnic groups as they grow older.

Given that there is no cure for the brittle bone but can only be maintained, considering the fragility of the bones of an OI baby, I STRONGLY speak against these kinds of treatment in all terms possible. I believe grandmothers can be useful, playing a crucial role in the support of care like exercises recommended by their professional caregiver, which will help improve the muscles and mobility of the child, thereby increasing the quality of life as the child grows into adulthood. Grandparents can also help with respite, assist with hospital appointments, administration of recommended medications when needed, and providing emotional support after corrective surgery or in the occurrence of a break. They can also assist by making financial contributions towards the child's treatment, especially if the grandparents are working and can.

In children with severe cases who requires a wheelchair or crutches, the availability of a strong support network throughout the child's life is critical, brittle bone children need respite, care, support, and attention throughout their lives, even though grandmothers know traditional methods, they can be trained in modern ways and procedures for safe handling, first aid and safeguarding the child.

Given the demands of our civilised society, I strongly believe that working parents can ask grandparents to babysit brittle bone children after providing the appropriate training and appropriate techniques required to safely carry out these babysitting duties.

My Opinion:

From my experience, and as a qualified Massage therapist, I will strongly recommend that this type of treatment or any form of massage treatment should NOT be given to a child with the brittle bone condition due to the fragility of their bones; from the basis of long-lasting culture and tradition, I know most grandmothers will disagree. The mother of the child can often find herself in a difficult position to object to these long-lasting traditions and the predicament she finds herself; therefore, if it must be rendered as I understand that this is a long-time tradition and cultural practice by our parents which has been passed down from generations, therefore, the grandma should adopt effleurage Massage at the lightest form of it hopefully, the grandma will eventually see the need to stop such form of treatment/care.

Effleurage, a French word meaning "to skim" or "to touch lightly on," is a series of massage strokes used in Swedish massage to warm up the muscle before applying deep tissue work using petrissage. This is a gentle, stroking movement used at the beginning and end of the facial and body massage, but for babies with OI, the strokes will be in the lightest form than when given to an adult.

I do not recommend massage for a child with the brittle bone condition due to fragility of the bones to avoid further fracture and damage to the child except done by a professional baby masseuse with tremendous and in-depth knowledge of Osteogenesis Imperfecta (OI). You only need to gently go over the baby's body, like blending the baby's body lotion or oil with the baby's body after the bath.

As a qualified massage therapist, I understand that massage itself has its benefits, just to name a few.

- With each light, gentle stroke, it helps the baby feel nurtured and loved.
- It helps to strengthen the bond between the mum and baby.
- Light stroke massage will also allow your baby to feel more relaxed, which may improve their sleep.
- It helps the flow of blood.
- It helps to relax the tension on muscles.

In some severe type cases, fractures could be detected during grandma's care, crispy sounds in the bones could be heard and felt. If you think you are going over an uncomfortable bump on the bone, all messages need to be stopped at that point, and the child should be taken to the hospital for further checks and tests for OI. Naturally, babies should feel comfortable and not cry with this type of light strokes massage but if the baby is highly uncomfortable and crying excessively combined with the above, that can be an indicator for further checks for oi by a qualified professional for a proper and clear diagnosis.

-Grandma care is also well-known and practiced traditionally in Sri- Lanka but this is not only limited to grandmas, a lot of relatives also perform stretches and massage on new-borns or infants, most of which are done in ignorance. Families do not do this to hurt the child and damage are done in ignorance as they do not know the complications of these massages to a child with OI or a disability.

Lifetime damages and complications arise from the ignorance and traditional beliefs which causes a child with disabilities and their family to be treated badly, shamed, and pushed out their communities. Some children are abandoned due to the belief that the child might be demonic.

-There is still stigma attached to disabilities, children with disabilities, and their family's needs to be protected and included even though is still a huge subject that definitely needs addressing in African countries and globally. We must understand that this issue causes mental health problems.

Massage is actually not necessary but has surely become a part of a tradition which has been passed down from generations as a practice for new mothers and their babies administered by elder women in the family and grandmas.

My experience with grandma's care/treatment:

"Ignorance is a DISEASE, but knowledge is POWER"

I will do my best to describe my experience, which will stay with me my whole life; I sometimes have shivers running down my spine when I think about it; flashback to the day when my son Steven was born. We were discharged from the hospital two days after his birth; on reaching home, I handed him over to my mother in law who was already at our home, she had already prepared food, awaiting our arrival from the hospital; after some few hours after we arrived, the preparation for care was started, an item that was arranged and put out was, a big bath bowl and a small bowl with lukewarm water in it, with a flannel or face towel as others may know it by, used to dab, wash and sometimes used to massage the baby's body, a kettle of hot water, soap, sponge, cream, comb for the baby's hair, towel, a lit-up lantern which is left on through the bath time and used at the end of bath time to care for the umbilical cord of the baby to aid healing..... that, I call another ritual all together on its own.

INTRODUCTION

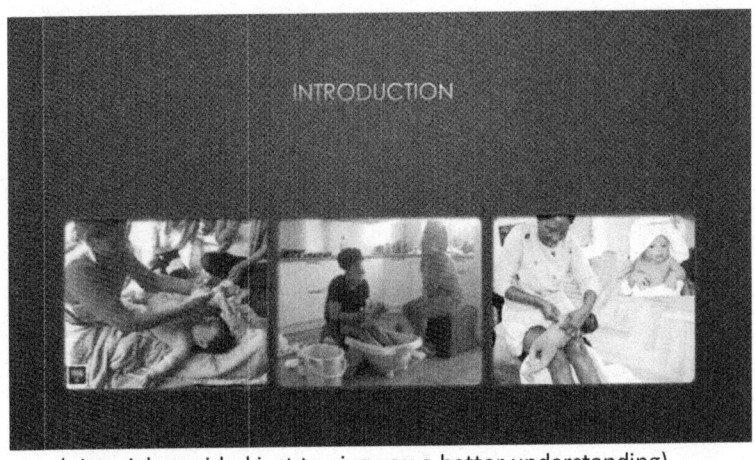

(pictorial provided just to give you a better understanding).

This kind of care treatment and practice is **STRONGLY NOT** advisable for babies with brittle bone (OI) conditions.

After using soap, water, and a sponge to wash, the baby's body is mopped with the towel, then the oil or cream is applied to the child... Hmmm.... that is when the massage is given with deep, heavy, and vigorous pressure with the tip of the grandma's fingers running deep through the body of the baby with much concentration on the joints, long bones, muscles, and nerves of the new-born as it is believed that the baby has been in a curved position in the womb for a long time just I have explained in my previous chapter, as they aim to straighten and stretch out the baby's muscles and nerves for better growth forgetting that the bones are fragile and prone to fracture even without any force.

The pulling of the arm can cause dislocation and loss of joints in an oi baby, which can be excruciatingly painful for anyone and even worse on a child with such a condition. The deep pressure of massage given can practically break every bone on the baby; pulling and lifting of the child by the head-up can curse the cervical vertebrae to disjoin or snap, leading to even more significant medical problems.

While this treatment was given to my son, he cried as he was in excruciating pain. I was very uncomfortable with the cry, so was my mother-in-law, but we thought he would stop with time. Unfortunately, we were so very wrong.

Steven cried continuously for hours afterward without stopping; during this care, we could hear weird and crispy sounds as my mother-in-law continued with the massage and care without knowing that my son's bones were cracking and breaking in several places. IGNORANCE.......

The same process of care and treatment was repeated the next morning; I was totally and intensely uncomfortable with the cry of my baby; halfway through the care/ treatment, my mother-in-law had to stop, dressed him up, and asked my husband and I to get ready, demanded that we take him

(Steven) to the hospital as she feels something was not right, Steven's femur on both legs was shorter than usual, swollen and she could feel bumps when she ran her hands and fingers down his legs. We also noticed that Steven did not move his legs and would surely cry by any lifting whatsoever.

When I had my son, I knew something was not quite right, all though, I could not place a finger on what was wrong; the doctors did not know exactly what the problem was even though it seemed apparent that he looked different with shorter and swollen limbs at birth; I was troubled, unhappy and cried all through this time, the pain was so unbearable.

We took Steven back to the hospital to see the doctor again; after a proper examination, the doctor recommended we go for ex-rays, behold! that was where we found out that Steven had six fractures on both legs. With all of these, I am glad that the doctor did not compound our problems by thinking we had done something terrible to the child even though there is a huge problem of ignorance and negligence as it relates to childhood disability across the globe.

There is also a problem of stigma in the society in Africa, Asian nations, even in the western world. Parents and family members with a disability need support. Support groups for children and families of children with OI are significant, a discussion around disabilities and support worldwide. This is a rare condition and requires more awareness. Families with children with a disability also suffer emotionally, physically, and mentally and need support to get them through tough times. There is a need for support at different levels through a multidisciplinary approach, set up to manage these children and their families.

Knowledge is key therefore joining support peer groups is helpful; sharing knowledge and experiences is also helpful, as this can be a good way for shifting from denial to accepting your child's disability which can, therefore, lead to safeguarding the child's best interest.

I believe this can also help improve the relationship dynamics of the child with their family, and their entire community. The grandma is undoubtedly needed as it makes respite easier and affordable for the family as they might not have to pay for her services, therefore, saving as the treatment for brittle bone disease can be very expensive especially in countries where the total cost of health care is paid by individuals and no contribution from the government.

Negative and ill-treatment of children can be dated as far back as the day of Mary Slessor's - the killing of the twins, as they were seen as evil children therefore treated as such. Many beliefs from a long time ago have shaped the way childhood disability is looked at in Nigeria and other countries. Our mission is to keep raising awareness to change the set down traditions and beliefs of people regarding disability. To dis-abuse minds from all these traditional beliefs that a child with a disability is evil and not useful to themselves, their families, and the society at large. Every child is a gift from God, even if born with any form of illness or disability.

In Nigeria, Kenya, many African and Asian countries, not much is known about OI yet even within the medical practice. There is still a stigma around OI; parents of children with OI still do not want anyone to know their children have OI, any form of disability or deformity due to fear of being shamed, stigmatized, ridiculed, and labeled, fear of being ostracized from their families and the society, again, this needs to change. This is the fear that I referred to in chapter two, where I spoke about FEAR. I didn't go through such, but I was told by very close friends to go dump my child with my mother in law in the village; I was told the city was not meant for children like my son that breaks all the time and in their term "normal" but thank goodness I didn't, as I could not understand or rationalize the sense in what they were talking about, this is my flesh and blood for goodness sake, in my opinion, this level of ignorance is disturbing and more needs to be done to create and raise brittle bone and disability awareness in our localities, Africa and across the globe.

Such kinds of stigma and words have the potentials to break any mother, but I remained strong, in my brokenness I believed someday things will change for good for us.
Postpartum visits for the mother and child to the hospital should also be encouraged by the grandmother and medical practitioners for early diagnosis and follow-up. The castigation of the woman with a child with a disability should also be discouraged, which is a common trend of the African and Asian society, like calling the mother a witch.

Training sessions for rural mothers and grandmothers on the proper safe handling of a child are recommended to ensure that the new-born is handled with great loving care, even if the child has OI and has not been diagnosed or has complications, fractures or not, safe handling should be practiced. Educating the grandmas on the proper secure handling of a new-born can also facilitate the spread of these teachings to other grandmas and mothers who would be grandmas in their later years.

Therefore, it is highly recommended that low expectations are not set for children with disabilities; neither should there be a limitation on what children with disabilities can do. It is good to raise them to be able to do all things possible.

It is also great for children with disabilities to be safeguarded from physical abuse no matter how well-meaning they are; some traditions beat children with disabilities because they believe these children have an evil spell on them, this views by some societies on disabilities need to be changed and I believe it can be done through education to avoid children with disabilities viewing themselves as mistakes following how they are treated. I would also recommend changing how the children are related to or referred to. It is important to refer to them by their name and not by the disability, they are first individuals and humans and should be treated as such.

Education is needed at all levels in our societies across the globe, both rural and urban, the way you treat your children with disability is the way others would see and treat them too, the way you work with them is the way others would work with them too, if you accept and love your child, the society will do the same just as the saying goes "charity begins at home." So, let the change start with you.

It is essential to ensure all tertiary institutions worldwide have a team that can work with children with OI and their families, adopting a multidisciplinary approach to help connect the dots in care on all levels. We cannot disenfranchise the grandmas, but we can educate them on letting them know that massage is unnecessary for babies with OI.

Awareness for OI is necessary with attention paid to the cries, facial cues, and bodily expression of the infant to which seeking good, Immediate, proper treatment and management for any form of disability are very necessary to help the family, friends in the support groups for mothers and children. Depending on the kind of condition, support is highly needed and recommended, it is essential to know that physiotherapy is also necessary for the development and care of the oi child.

As well as integrating the child into society starts from the home, which can be achieved with the support of families, including grandmas and grandpas.

CHAPTER 6
BELIEF AND FAITH

CHAPTER 6
BELIEF AND FAITH

Most society is big on spiritual backing for everything, and a lot of things get over spiritualized in our society including the African and Asian communities. I strongly believe these need to be changed, and change can only come again, through much awareness and education. It is imperative at this point to make it clear that Osteogenesis Imperfecta, aka brittle bone disease, is a medical condition. Period. It is a genetic condition, a **disorder** that results in **fragile bones** that break easily. It is typically presented at birth, and it develops in children who have a family history of the **disease** but sometimes can happen through mutation. NOW... what is a mutation?

The mutation is the changing of the structure of a gene, resulting in a variant form that may be transmitted to subsequent generations, caused by the alteration of single base units in DNA, or the deletion, insertion, or rearrangement of larger sections of genes or chromosomes. if this happens then it is known as "imperfectly formed **bone**."

I believe it is wrong to stigmatize children with disabilities. It is inappropriate to name-calling them, e.g., like an evil child. Believing that they are witches just because they are not in your own words, "Normal".

Psalm 127 has a verse that says, "Children are an inheritance from the Lord, a reward from him," which does not only apply to children without disabilities but for all children, including children with any form of disability, including OI.

The Bible also says we can do all things through Christ that strengthens us, so, therefore, living and raising a child with a disability, God knows why and would surely give the needed strength for it. We all have our purpose of existence in life, whether with or without disability, I believe we should accept, respect, and love them, regardless of our difference in race, ability, age, or color, ability, or disability.
John 9:1-3 talks about a man who was born blind, and there were conversations on why he was blind, if it was because of the sins of his parents or his fault, and Jesus says no, it is not anyone's fault. The Bible also shows how much Jesus treated people with disabilities as individuals and as people with emotions. There is nowhere in the Bible that children with disabilities are devils or their parents did something wrong.

Making them feel they are the worst human on earth and feeling condemned is definitely not right and totally ungodly and should not be encouraged in any form, manner, or level.

Many people have gone through many difficulties, trials, temptations from friends, families, and society as a whole; most has let them down, especially from people they are very close to who is supposed to support them, hold their hand through the dark times, people that they rely on and trusted have contributed either negatively or positively to their faith. It can be helpful for you to know that many have passed through this before you, and they came out on the other side stronger.

During my time of pain and agony, where friends would even say to me that my son was evil and some would say to me that I must have sinned against God, he is punishing me for my sins by giving me a child-like Steven as a penance for my sins against him, hmmm... my goodness... is this ever true? Some would even go as far as saying it must be the sin of my father and forefathers raining down on me and I needed deliverance from that cause, some cleansing because he was born with a broken bone and could do nothing but cry all day long due to fractured bone pain he was having.

They also recommended where best to go for such deliverance, which they offered to take me with my son there themselves. That broke my heart even more; such comments made me look deep inside; it made me assessed myself deeper to determine if I have truly sinned. Some even believe that he was a reincarnation of someone who died in a ghastly motor accident and has come back to re-live his life as my son hence the broken bone at birth. Hmmm.... dear goodness, just imagine the effect of such a statement in such a time of pain, distress, and agony.

"If they hadn't tried to break me down, I wouldn't know that I'm unbreakable".

Gabourey Sidibe

Some of my close friends even asked me if I went anywhere fetish to seek a child, Now- I found that statement very strange. This statement came from the deepest of tradition, culture, belief and shows the mindset of people. Those comments had a profound impact on me for a very long while; they made me become desperate for help and cure for my son without even knowing what exactly the problem was as we had not had a diagnosis by then, it brought indescribable fear and shame to the extent that I could not freely bring my child out to the street or public places anymore.

I have spoken to a few African OI mothers and found out that the same goes for them. Again, I believe, this has to do with tradition and culture. This type of tradition, culture, belief, and mindset of people must be changed because it does more damage and no good to both the mother, the child, and the family.

Steven grew older in age but extremely slow, and he did not increase in weight and size, which is one of the qualities of brittle bone disease, which means he wore the same size of clothing, diaper for a longer time, unlike his peers. I could remember when he was three, I sent my younger brother to get me some diaper from the corner shop where we lived. I requested size one of pampers which is for new-born babies. He came back to me saying - shop owner was asking why he was buying a baby diaper, and if we had a new baby in the house; suddenly, I felt more profound shame. At that point, I lost the remaining confidence I had left, I busted in uncontrollable tears in deep sadness, agony, and deep pain, and that made me question my faith and believe in God and wondered if God truly loves me, I also wondered why he would not do anything to bring me out of this pain, Mistry, and deep shame, why he will not heal my son despite all my faith I have in him.

Over the years, I took strong courage from the story of Job in the Bible, who, according to the Bible, was a man that was right before God. He lost everything, his children, his riches, and all that he had, including his friend who said to him that God was punishing him because of his sin; they insisted and believed that Job's suffering was a result of his sin even though Job himself asserted he has not sinned against God and expressed his unshakable confidence in God, his friends deserted and forsook him, they judged and condemned him even before the God they claimed he had sinned against. The job was able to stand firm on his word, his belief, and faith because he knows he had not sinned, and God will not punish him like that because of sin as he knew that God is not a wicked God, so he kept trusting in him.

Man is so quick to judge and condemn because they are too short-sighted. I also strongly believe that ignorance of who God is and the true word of God regarding situations in our lives come into play here, but Job did not give up and held on strong, stayed focused and positive. (Book of Job in the Bible) At the end of it, all God restored all that Job had lost in multiple folds, which was the same in my case and I give him glory every day for that.

I am strongly encouraged by the book of Job, and I knew straight away that there is a brighter tomorrow for my son Steven and I, I knew things can get better, and that strengthened my faith. Knowing the word for myself made a huge difference in both my life and my son's. I was able to see for myself who God really is, his WILL for me. That made me not stand for any negative, superstitious beliefs and rubbish talks from anyone anymore, not even from close friends which changed my perspective, orientation, and mindset, Yes, sometimes their words got to me which is the same with everyone but picking myself up again is what matters, that is what makes the difference.

At that point, I felt I had enough, and I had reached a point in my life that I had to make a conscious decision not to allow anyone to tell me or suggest to me what they think, believe or what they believe the Bible says because their interpretations of the bible were not the truth. I call it "KNOW GOD FOR YOURSELF", which made a huge difference in my life.

Religious Jargons:

Most people believe far more in their pastors than the word itself, following blindly and accepting every word that comes out of whoever calls himself a man of God without reasoning nor questioning what is not right even when it does not make sense to them. Most churches and pastors have taken advantage of people's ignorance and respect for God to keep families and carers, especially women, under abuse, bondage, and extortion.

It is important to stress that God never condemned or judged people with disability in the Bible; instead, he accepted them, supported, healed, and then set them on their way to freedom; therefore, understanding this will help individuals move past seeking miracles from their pastors. Understanding that God is a miracle worker and not a magician can help one know and value patience, completely trusting in Him and not running to every miracle house or centre you hear off seeking for what is not true.

It is religious jargon and complete lies to say children with a disability are from the devil, and therefore they are not to be seen publicly or even accepted in the church. It is wrong to make a mother and her child with a disability go through vigorous pain all in the name of deliverance, trying to cast the devil and demons out of them. For example, just because a child is blind, cannot walk, nor speak, nor do things of his or her peers can do makes the child evil or different, it might be nothing but a slight delay in development.

In my opinion, every person is disabled in one way or form as your strength might be someone else's weakness and vies vassal. Name-calling and labeling should not be tolerated or acceptable.

Every person living with a brittle bone disease or other forms of disability and their carers can find life much easier, blossom if people can simply change their mindset. It is important to understand those religious jargons are not needed so break free from it so you can live in freedom.

CHAPTER 7

The Enrichment of Vitamin D

CHAPTER 7
The Enrichment of Vitamin D

Vitamin D has been an essential and lifesaving vitamin for us. Before Pamidronate is administered every three months or Zoledronic Acid infusion every six months, my son would have to do a Vitamin D level test to determine the level of his Vit D in his system, which also allows the doctors to decide whether he has the right amount of Vit D in or if he needs a top-up, this is so important especially as a dark-skinned child in a country where the people are not very much exposed to sunlight and so difficult to absorb enough Vit D through the sun.

In the UK, there is hardly enough sun through the Autumn and winter months, making it even more essential to take Vitamin D tablets to keep him at the right level his body needs.

Vitamin D helps regulate the amount of calcium and phosphate in the body. The nutrients are needed to keep bones, teeth, and muscles healthy, which Steven needs, as brittle bone disease, affects his teeth, as teeth are part of the bone. Do you also know that lack of vitamin D can lead to bone deformities such as rickets in children and bone pain caused by a condition called osteomalacia in adults? Insufficient vitamin D can also lead to fragile bones prone to more breakage. The nutrient aids the body in absorbing calcium, which is essential to healthy bones, and fertility problems.

Vitamin D can also help to improve the problem with (DI) dental Imperfecta, which is also seen among people who suffer from brittle bone condition (OI), which my son Steven also suffers from and has to be checked out regularly by a qualified dentist, over the years my son Steven has suffered from over a hundred fracture and more, we have stopped counting now, he has had successful four major orthopedic rodding corrective surgeries on both longs at both Great Ormond Street Hospital for children in London and Stanmore Orthopaedic Hospital all here in the UK, Before all of these could happen, it was essential to keep an eye on his vitamin D level.

The Shriners Hospital in America has also done fantastic research on these, and I thought it would be great to add it on for your read.

Check Vitamin D Level in Children Having Orthopedic Surgery:

Vitamin D has been in the news a lot lately. Are we getting enough? Should we take supplements? What about people who cannot get enough sunshine to make vitamin D needed for bone health? And what about children? What are "normal" levels of vitamin D for them?

This study from the Shriners Hospital for Children in Texas addresses concerns about vitamin D levels in children having bone surgery. The goal was to find out how much vitamin D children had who were admitted for orthopedic surgery. Measurements were taken from blood samples of 70 children ages two to 19 years old before surgery.

Vitamin D helps regulate calcium absorption from the gut (gastrointestinal tract). Calcium is an essential ingredient in strong bones. The skin makes vitamin D but relies on sun exposure to do so. With so much time spent indoors and lower sunlight levels year-round in the northern hemispheres, many children around the world have either vitamin insufficiency or deficiency.

The difference between insufficiency and deficiency is a matter of degree. Vitamin D insufficiency is defined as a blood level of 25-hydroxyvitamin-D (25 OHD) that falls below 32 ng/mL. 25 OHD is a chemical compound that must be present in the body for vitamin D to be made. It is called a precursor (comes before) chemical.

Vitamin D deficiency occurs when 25 OHD levels fall below 20 ng/mL. The levels for insufficiency and deficiency are determined by another factor — and that is the amount of 25 OHD needed to keep parathyroid levels in the normal range. Without going into the complex physiology of the body to explain the interactions between the hormonal systems, suffice it to say that vitamin D levels and parathyroid function are intimately linked together.

Other risk factors for decreased vitamin D include obesity, increased skin pigmentation (dark skin), older age, and not enough vitamin D in the diet. Children with metabolic bone disorders such as osteogenesis imperfecta (weak and brittle bones) and rickets are at a much greater risk for poor bone healing, which can be compounded by low vitamin D levels.

Finding out preoperative levels of vitamin D may be important because bone healing after fractures and surgical procedures depends on sufficient levels of vitamin D. To look for other factors that might affect vitamin D levels and/or bone healing, the researchers conducting this study also gathered additional information on each patient.

Age, sex (male or female), ethnicity, body mass index (BMI), diagnosis, and geographic location (where they normally lived: the United States or Mexico) were included in the sampling. Vitamin D levels collected were also compared to the season.

They found that African American children were at the greatest risk for vitamin D deficiency. As shown in other studies, vitamin D levels were at their lowest during the winter season. Age and ethnicity combined was a major risk factor. For example, African Americans between the ages of 12 and 19 years old were 20 times more likely to be vitamin D deficient compared with Caucasians (whites). Seasonal levels of vitamin D did fluctuate with lower levels measured in the winter.

There was no obvious or statistically significant link between vitamin D levels and type of orthopedic diagnosis or body mass index (BMI). The kinds of orthopedic conditions children were treated for included scoliosis and other spine problems, cerebral palsy, hip dysplasia, leg length difference, and other (unspecified) orthopedic (bone) problems. (Study by Shriners Hospital).

Benefits of Vitamin D on children with oi:

Generally, it is good for the human body; Osteogenesis Imperfecta (OI), aka brittle bone disease, is a defect where collagen (the protein that is responsible for bone structure) is missing, reduced, or of low quality, so it is not enough to support the minerals in the bone which makes the bone weak, in turn causing the bones to easily fracture. Vitamin D can aid the support and strengthening of a child's bone.

Vitamin D is an important nutrient that is essential to our health. It boosts immunity, keeps bones strong and skin healthy, stimulates cell growth, and helps create new hair follicles. Often called the 'sunshine vitamin', vitamin D plays an integral role in skin protection and rejuvenation. In its active form as calcitriol, vitamin D contributes to skin cell growth, repair, and metabolism. It enhances the skin's immune system and helps to destroy free radicals that can cause premature aging.

Vitamin D helps the body absorb calcium and phosphorus from the food you eat. So, the nutrient is important for people with osteoporosis. Studies show that calcium and vitamin D together can build stronger bones in women after menopause. It also helps with other disorders that cause weak bones, like rickets, and several extensive research studies have shown that taking vitamin D decreases the risk of fractures. This includes foot and ankle fractures as well as other fractures, such as hip and wrist fractures. Improved fracture healing has also been found in people taking vitamin D.

Benefits of vitamin D in children with dark skin:

In the western countries where sunlight varies, darker skin tones tend to suffer from a vitamin D deficiency. Our bodies cannot absorb calcium, magnesium, and phosphate essential for maintaining strong bones and teeth without it. People with dark skin, such as African, African-Caribbean, or south Asian origin, will need to spend longer in the sun to produce the same amount of vitamin D as someone with lighter skin.

Some people are at greater risk of vitamin D deficiency, including People with naturally very dark skin. This is because the pigment (melanin) in dark skin does not allow the skin to absorb UV radiation.

Symptoms of low vitamin D in the body.
What are the signs and symptoms of vitamin D deficiency?
Fatigue.
Bone pain.
Muscle weakness, muscle aches, or muscle cramps.
Mood changes, like depression. Etc

So, it is advisable to take vitamin D. Current guidelines say adults should not take more than the equivalent of 100 micrograms a day. But vitamin D is a 'fat-soluble' vitamin, so your body can store it for months, and you do not need it every day and I will recommend you speak to your physician to advance you on dosage for YOU if you are not sure.

CHAPTER 8
Family Support

CHAPTER 8
Family Support

Dealing with disability itself can be challenging and sometimes traumatizing. It is very important and helpful to have a family support network around you, to hold your hands, lift you and encourage you from time to time as needed.

As mentioned earlier, my family are Christians, very supportive, accepted my child who always breaks bones and cries all the time without knowing its cause. They were very understanding and helpful in every way you can think of. I am so grateful that I had such an amazingly supportive and compassionate family, which eased my burden, imagine what my position would have been if the reverse was the case or the trauma it would have gone through, I could remember so many time having my sister coming over to give me a helping hand with house chores, cooking and caring for my older son, giving me time to take care of my younger son Steven and rest if possible. I accepted every offer of help I could get as I needed it at that time.

So many times, I have released that it is so difficult for some of us that find ourselves in such a predicament as mine, find it extremely difficult to ask or accept help when it is being offered because they see it as weakness on their part ... If you ask me, no person is a superhero in this circumstance, we all require support and help at one point or another, so, if you need help ask for it, accept it when offered you because it will do you good in the long run.

In all of this drama in our Life, you would ask, where was my extended family? What role did they play in our lives? Did I receive any support? Hmmm.... what an excellent question to ask at these points in time. The answer to that question is, "Yes", I did receive a hundred percent support from my extended family; my sister-in-law and my niece will take turns to come over to mine, stay for weeks and sometimes for months, sometimes I would go over to my dad's. My in-laws were incredibly supportive, and they never gave me any problems whatsoever, they often came over to help, as mentioned in my previous chapter how my mother-in-law had come over, prepared food awaiting our arrival from the hospital, how she prepared to give care to Steven and how she noticed the fractures on Steven and asked us to take him back to the hospital for further examination. Wow! What an amazing woman she is?

It is very important and extremely helpful when you have a supportive family and your in-laws at any given time, no matter the situation or circumstance around it, especially when raising a child with a disability to help you transition through life successfully, without which can be extremely stressful and difficult.

African culture/disability and women:

In African culture, where disability is looked upon like a turbo, you will always be at the receiving end as a woman. Society has a culture where you as a woman is blamed for everything that goes wrong in the home including having a child with a disability. In worse scenarios, the woman can be called names. Most time, the family of the husband will be against her; they can also pressurise their son to leave the marriage, abandon the woman and the kids, they can even go to the extent of finding another wife for their son, claiming the wife is evil with her child which they will not want anything to do with her. I have seen cases where the woman and the child/ren are ostracize and some women devoiced by their husbands all because they bore children with deformity or disability, they become outcast and lose everything.

This treatment has made many women have a nervous breakdown, anxiety, depression, mental issues, and many more.

My experience:

I feel blessed because I never had to go through such extra pain and trauma especially dealing with my son's condition. The love, help, and support I received from my family helped me find time for rest at intervals to help me re-energize to resume my caring role when needed, however, it was not easy to leave him alone for long hours with anyone in the first few years of birth, but every little time I could get to catch my breath of fresh air or sleep was very much needed and appreciated, now that things are a lot better, and I am exceptionally grateful and glad I had that support, my husband was incredible as we were in it together and took turns at night caring for Steven.

I can remember having to go stay at my family home for weeks, to receive help, also allow my husband quality time of rest for work because we somehow have to earn money for bills. I remember Steven crying nights after night not able to sleep, we will try to catch some sleep during the day and my dad would come over to our room, all covered in tears, kneeling by our bedside gently praying in my native language, that touched and strengthen me a lot. Thank you, dad...

At this point, I must not forget to mention, one of the things that helped me over the years, which is my network and support group, a network that became part of my family: my church, Bethany Community Church led by Neil and Sonya Chitty, with outstanding members. The level and measure of love I received were indescribable and unquantifiable, I had never experienced such in my entire life. It is important to mention and acknowledge all these amazing people in our journey without which life may have gone another direction which I might I found it so difficult to cope with. Their impact on our lives has been tremendous, which has put us in a perfect place where we can now comfortably accept our fate and continue our life's journey.

Bethany's vision is to be a community that radically loves God and others, bringing transformation locally, nationally, and globally. The church is a charismatic Christian community of people of all ages, cultures, and walks of Life; Bethany believes in one God: Father, Son, and Holy Spirit; they believe Jesus died to pay for our sins and was raised again and through faith in him we are adopted by grace as sons and daughters of amazing Father God as he fills us with his Holy

Spirit to go and share His good news throughout the world. This is what I believe in too. It felt right, which was contrary to what some friends have said to me in the past, that my son's condition and disability is not because of either my sins or my father's sins (Generational Sin) which is exactly what the Bible teaches, at Bethany, my son was first seen before the disability and was identified and addressed as a person "Steven" first, and not the disability. Which should be the case and not the other way round.

One of the things that also blew my mind away got me more attracted to Bethany Community Church: their culture, again, was utterly the opposite of most African culture, traditions, and belief "if you don't set culture the culture will set itself". This is the culture of HONOUR, AUTHENTICITY, ACCEPTANCE, COURAGE, GENEROSITY; these five areas of their culture worked so well for me, my family, for Bethany, and their community again, was what I needed to help me heal, move forward, and experience complete freedom.

The church also feels that God is at work across the nations; they connect through relationships with individuals, churches around the world as well as in the UK; they also love to support and learn from one another and cheer each other on to greatness without being judgemental or discriminative of anyone. We felt welcomed, unconditionally loved, and wholly accepted without being labeled or shamed; we felt connected, again, was the type of environment I needed to help me heal and move on; you can see the huge difference in both beliefs, cultures, even the mindset of people both here in the UK and Africa.

Talking about Family, I must not fail to mention the Brittle Bone Society UK, founded by the late Margret Grant, now headed by Patricia Osborne; the organization has also been another network just like a real family in this journey of ours, I am so very grateful for their countless support without which life would have been so tough. I gained tons and a wealth of tremendous knowledge through the BBS conferences, which also gave me the strength to carry on, knowing what the condition is all about mad a huge difference in our lives. Knowing where to find help, managing, and giving adequate care to my lovely baby boy Steven, who was three and a half then. Having a great measure of understanding of brittle bone made a huge and tremendous difference; it threw so much light on my part, definitely "It pays to gain knowledge".

Life itself can be so difficult; having a child or children with brittle bone conditions or any other form of disability makes life even more difficult and complicated. Yes, life can be unfair; it is a journey which sometimes you must take baby steps at a time; life's experiences can crush one, but with the right network, the right help, and the right people around you, it can certainly be easier.

I know it is so difficult for some people to accept help. They cannot ask for help when they need one, I was humble enough to ask for help many times, and accept it when It is been offered, I have no regrets whatsoever for accepting, it has helped me a lot in life so, I will encourage to do same if you need it.

encourage to do same if you need it.
"That which does not kill you makes you stronger".
Never give up; you can make it. Have the UNBREAKABLE Spirit.

Conclusion:

Even as we find ourselves in this unprecedented time, family support is inevitable. The importance of family (network) cannot be overemphasised, we all need one another to laugh, play, cry, chat, and love, to do things together, remember, as the saying goes "no man is an island".

These times have proven to us that families/networks cannot and should not be replaced or taken for granted but we must do everything in our power to keep family (network) together for this is the support system that will help you keep mind, body, and soul together.

Personally, I am so grateful for my families, (networks), it has kept me going, and can successfully fight through the isolation, mental instability, and more that have come with this pandemic. I know that it has been a bit of an unpredictable year and the pandemic has thrown some difficult things our way, but I also know that God has been on the move and doing great things as he is my faithfulness and my anchor to the ground which makes me unshakeable, unmovable, and unbreakable.

"Never allow yourself to break, but always remain unbreakable. …"

www.tarelaaghanti.com

Printed in Great Britain
by Amazon